For Jacob and Boyd who love the ocean, big fish, and good stories. —T. B.

For my lovely family—Alex, Lily Peach, and Rudy George. —J.

Text copyright © 2012 by Tilda Balsley
Illustrations copyright © 2012 by Lerner Publishing Group, Inc.

KAR-BEN Publishing
A division of Lerner Publishing Group, Inc.
241 First Avenue North
Minneapolis, MN 55401 U.S.A.
1-800-4KARBEN

Website address: www.karben.com

Library of Congress Cataloging-in-Publication Data

Balsley, Tilda.
      Oh no, Jonah! / by Tilda Balsley ; illustrated by Jago.
         p.   cm.
      ISBN 978-0-7613-5139-9 (lib. bdg. : alk. paper)
      1. Jonah (Biblical prophet)—Juvenile literature. 2. Bible stories, English—
O.T. Jonah. I. Jago. II. Jonah and the whale. III. Title.
      BS580.J55B35 2012
      224'.9209505—dc23   2011029038

Manufactured in the United States of America
1 – PC – 12/31/11

Oh No, Jonah!

Tilda Balsley illustrations by Jago

KAR-BEN
PUBLISHING

God spoke to Jonah long ago:

"That Nineveh's a horror show.
Go preach to them, and let them know
Their wicked ways have got to go."

"Preach," said Jonah. "That's not fun—
Ragging, nagging everyone.
Who will thank me when I'm done?
I'll tell you who: Not even one.

"So that's a job I think I'll skip.
I'll hide from God. I'll take a trip
To Tarshish, on this sailing ship.
All aboard, now let her rip!"

Oh no, Jonah!

As the ship sailed off from shore,
The wind whipped up a fearful roar.
And drenching rain began to pour.
There'd never been such waves before.
Sailors sprawled across the floor.
They begged their gods:

"No more! No more!"

But Jonah heard no thunderclap.
He'd gone below to take a nap.
The sailors woke him up and said:

"This is no time to stay in bed.
You should be praying hard instead."

"Now let's draw straws and that will show
Whose fault this is. We need to know."

The sailors held their breath, then saw
That Jonah drew the shortest straw.
He raised his voice above the sound
Of angry ocean all around.

"The God who made both earth and sea
Has sent this storm because of me.
I'm a jinx you can't afford,
So please, just throw me overboard,
And peaceful seas will be restored."

The sailors gasped with one accord:

"The awful truth can't be ignored.
Let's act now before we crash.
One, two, three, heave ho, now SPLASH!"

Oh no, Jonah!

Immediately, the weather cleared.
But things were worse than Jonah feared.

"I wish I hadn't volunteered."

A giant fish swam to his side,
And stared at him all google-eyed.
Its mouth, humongous, opened wide,
And CHOMP!
He found himself inside.

Oh no, Jonah!

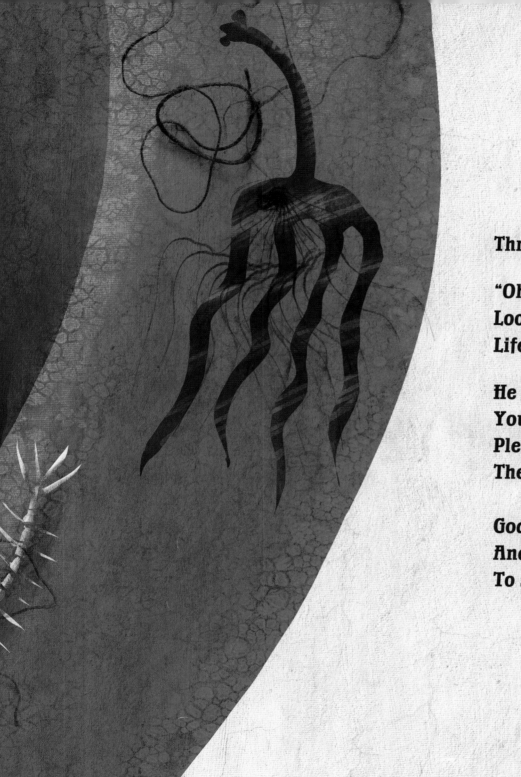

Three days and nights poor Jonah cried:

"Oh woe is me, I wish I'd died.
Look at this half-eaten stuff.
Life inside a fish is rough."

He prayed: "All right, God, fair enough.
You saved me from the sea, it's true—
Please save me from this big fish, too.
Then what you want is what I'll do."

God was quick to grant his prayer.
And whispered to the fish: "Take care
To spit the man out over there."

Then God sent Jonah on his way
And this time Jonah said okay.
He went to Nineveh that day.
He preached to them: "Like it or not,
Forty days is all you've got.
For God has doomed this wretched spot."

The poor, the rich, all ages heard.
The hearts of Nineveh were stirred.
The king said, "Let us pray and fast—
And turn from wickedness at last.
If we repent and pray for pity,
God may show mercy on our city."

So God spared every Ninevite.
But Jonah said: "This isn't right."

He yelled at God: "You're way too soft.
I knew you'd let those sinners off."

God wouldn't even hear him out:

"What are you so mad about?"

And Jonah went away to pout.

The sun beat down. He felt betrayed.

"Oh, for a sip of lemonade."

God grew a vine for cooling shade.
A slight breeze blew, it gently swayed.
And Jonah felt his anger fade.

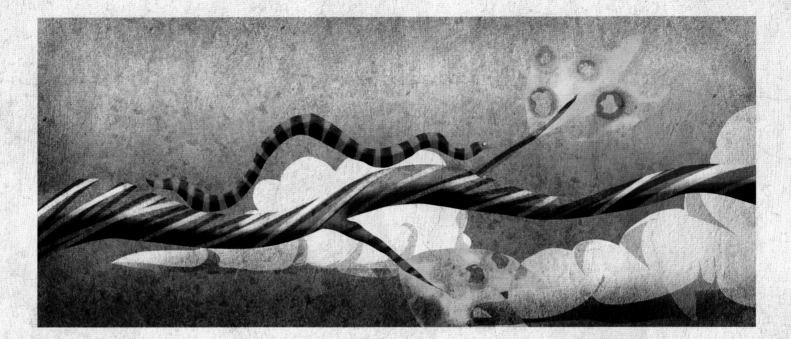

But soon the plant had holes all through it.
God had sent a worm to chew it.
By morning sweaty Jonah knew it.
He shouted at the God who grew it:

"My plant is gone. How could you do it?"

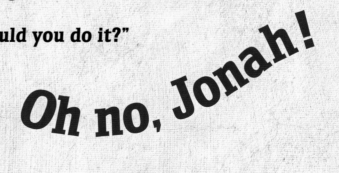

Oh no, Jonah!

God said:

"How dare you rave and rant?
You didn't even grow the plant.
The Ninevites have changed their ways
And well before the forty days.

I had, therefore, a change of heart
For Nineveh: a brand new start.
Why should that make you fall apart?"

The story ends right there and then.
A big fish tale from way back when,
Still telling us how we should live,
And showing us how to forgive.

About the Author

Tilda Balsley, with her signature rhyme, loves to bring Biblical tales to life. "The story of Jonah being swallowed by a gigantic creature captures the imagination of children and adults alike," she says. "For me, even a few big waves can be discombobulating!" Tilda and her husband live in Reidsville, North Carolina and like to spend time at the beach. Her previous books include *Let My People Go!*, *The Queen Who Saved Her People*, and *Maccabee!* (Kar-Ben).

About the Illustrator

Jago, a graduate of Falmouth College of Art, has illustrated over two dozen books for U.S. and U.K. publishers. His books include National Jewish Book Award Finalist *Nachshon, Who Was Afraid to Swim* (Kar-Ben). His first book *Fig's Giant* (Oxford University Press) was adapted by the BBC for a children's television series and also won a National Children's Literacy Association Award. He lives in North Cornwall, England.